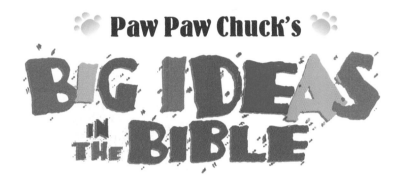

Paw Paw Chuck's
BIG IDEAS
IN THE BIBLE

Charles R. Swindoll
Illustrated by Ross Vera

WORD
kids!

WORD PUBLISHING
Dallas • London • Vancouver • Melbourne

Paw Paw Chuck's Big Ideas in the Bible

Text and art copyright © 1995 by Charles R. Swindoll.

Scripture quotations are from the *International Children's Bible, New Century Version*, copyright © 1983, 1986, 1988 by Word Publishing, Dallas, Texas 75234.

Illustrations are by Ross Vera through Rosenthal Represents, Los Angeles, California.

Managing Editor: Laura Minchew   Project Editor: Beverly Phillips

Library of Congress Cataloging-in-Publication Data
Swindoll, Charles R.
    Paw Paw Chuck's big idea's in the Bible / Charles R. Swindoll.
        p. cm.
        Summary: Stories telling how people in the Bible dealt with real-life troubles are followed by stories using bear characters and showing how young people today can find answers to their everyday struggles.
        ISBN 0-8499-1067-6
        [1. Christian life—Fiction. 2. Bears—Fiction. 3. Bible stories.] I. Title.
        PZ7.S98215Paw 1995
        [Fic]—dc20
                                                                95-24897
                                                                    CIP
                                                                    AC

Printed in the United States of America

95 96 97 98 99 00 RRD 9 8 7 6 5 4 3 2

DEDICATION

A big part of the reason this project
was so much fun to put together has been my
relationship with our eight wonderful "grandcubs."
Their paws are all over these pages!

It is only right, therefore,
that I dedicate this book to them.
I love each one with all my heart.

Ryan, Chelsea, and Landon Swindoll
Parker and Heather Nelson
Ashley and Austin Dane
and our "littlest cub" (so far) Noah Swindoll

FROM "PAW PAW CHUCK" TO PARENTS

A personal letter

Among Cynthia's and my most cherished memories are the hours we spent with our four children telling stories. She loved reading to them. I always preferred making up the stories from my imagination. Either way, our kids, especially in their younger years, enjoyed both.

As the years have passed, our "cubs" have grown up and become Papa and Mama bears with cubs of their own. Let me introduce our entire pack to you, including, of course, our eight "grandcubs":

- Curt, our oldest, married Debbie . . . and their three cubs are Ryan (11), Chelsea (10), and Landon (6).
- Charissa, next in order, married Byron . . . and they have two: Parker (9) and Heather (7).
- Colleen, four years younger than her sister, married Mark . . . and they now have two: Ashley (3) and Austin (1½).
- Chuck, our youngest, married Jeni . . . and they have our youngest grandcub, Noah (1).

What a fun bunch! And now *they* are the ones who are reading and telling the stories. Well, we do too, but not as often as before. Every time we do, however, I am amazed all over again at the impact a simple, carefully worded story can have on young lives. Nothing quiets them quicker or so completely captures their curiosity.

Some time ago—it must have been almost two years now—a creative thought entered my head. Why not write a storybook for children? But just another children's book wouldn't do. This one needed to be different . . . really unique.

Instead of its being either a fantasy-based series of imaginative stories or strictly a factual collection of stories from the Bible, why not blend the two? Furthermore, since kids of all ages love nature so much and since they seem to remember stories better when they're tied in with the animal world, I decided to illustrate my stories by using bears—soft, friendly, fuzzy bears. And while my creative juices were squirting, why not weave our eight little "grandcubs" into the stories? In fact, everything flowed best when everyone in the stories was portrayed in "bear" form, including "Paw Paw Chuck" and "Nana Cindy"!

You hold in your hands the result of those original thoughts. This is my very first attempt at putting some tasty theological cookies on the bottom shelf. Each story, as you will see, covers one main truth or theme based on one of the many major subjects found in God's Word.

To keep the interest level fully engaged, I have maintained the same child-friendly pattern: the beginning of an imaginary story from the lives of the bears, which leads into a situation or predicament any kid can identify with . . . then a true story from the Scriptures that fits into the same category or idea . . . followed by the ending of the story where a vital lesson of moral value is taught or some significant virtue is underscored.

My hope? That this colorful and cozy little book will bring you and your own "cubs" or "grandcubs" hours of pleasure together, prompting you to have ample opportunity to discuss many of the important things in life. By the way, don't forget to add a big bear hug as you finish each session. A good story without a hug is like a fragrant bouquet without a kiss or like a great big sundae without a cherry.

If you have half the fun reading these pages as I have had writing them, then my big ol' bear's heart will beat a little faster . . . and my paws might be tempted to scratch out more books similar to this one!

Chuck Swindoll

(ALIAS, "PAW PAW CHUCK")

CONTENTS

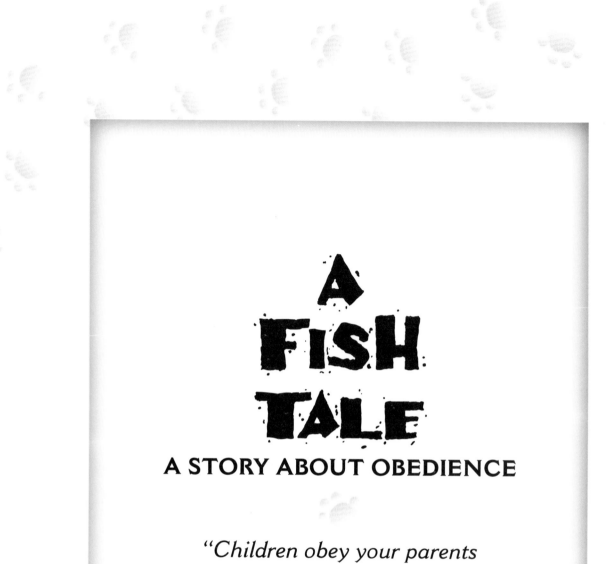

A FISH TALE

A STORY ABOUT OBEDIENCE

*"Children obey your parents
the way the Lord wants.
This is the right thing to do."*
EPHESIANS 6:1

"It's time to wash your paws and close your jaws," Paw Paw Chuck said with a smile.

"Aww . . . do we have to go to bed now?" Cubby complained. "Couldn't Buzzy and I stay up a little longer?"

"Cubby, I've allowed you and your friend Buzzy to play for two hours past your usual bedtime," Paw Paw Chuck kindly reminded him. "You must get some sleep, so you can get up early tomorrow morning to go fishing with me."

"Oh, yeah! Tomorrow's the big day! We love to fish!" the little bears squealed with delight as they jumped into bed. "We can 'bearly' wait!"

After the cubs said their prayers, Paw Paw Chuck hugged them and said, "Good night, Cubby. Good night, Buzzy. Please, go to sleep now."

"We will," Cubby promised.

But the minute Paw Paw Chuck left the room, Buzzy said, "Cubby, I have an idea. We don't have to wait until tomorrow to catch fish. Let's go fishing *tonight!*"

"What?" Cubby asked with surprise. "Paw Paw Chuck said we had to go to sleep. He won't let us step one paw outside the front door."

"Maybe not," Buzzy said, with a gleam in his eyes. "But who says we need to go out the door? We can sneak out your bedroom window. It's only a few paws high. C'mon!"

"I don't know," Cubby said thoughtfully. "Paw Paw Chuck said . . ."

"Oh, don't worry. We won't get caught. We'll be back before he knows we're gone," Buzzy assured him.

"Well, okay."

Quickly and quietly, the bears climbed out Cubby's bedroom window and plopped onto the soft grass below.

"It sure is dark out here," Cubby said, with fear in his voice.

"Shhhhhh!" Buzzy whispered loudly. "Don't make any noise. We don't want Paw Paw Chuck to hear us. Come on!" They stood up and "tip-pawed" around to the back porch.

Paw Paw Chuck had arrived earlier that day to stay with the cubs while Cubby's mother was out of town. Paw Paw Chuck had helped Cubby and Buzzy get their fishing poles and bait ready. They had placed three poles and three buckets of bait on the back porch.

Now, Cubby and Buzzy grabbed their poles and bait, and they ran out into the dark toward the pond, just beyond the house. The moon was out, but clouds kept floating across it. "Let's fish from our favorite spot on the old boat dock," Buzzy called over his shoulder, as he bounded onto the dock ahead of Cubby.

"Okay. But slow down, it's hard to see where I'm . . ."

Just then, as the cubs neared the end of the dock, Cubby tripped over a loose, wooden plank.

"Yee . . . ow!" Cubby cried. He stumbled and tumbled. SPLASH! Cubby dropped right into the pond! The water was cold and deep.

"Help! Help!" Cubby yelled. "Throw me the rope, Buzzy."

"I can't find it!" called Buzzy. The clouds were blocking the moonlight. "It's too dark to see anything!"

Cubby was not a strong swimmer, and his fur soaked up water like a thick rug. He soon began to sink. "Help! Help!" he cried again, just before his head bobbed below the water. Cubby slapped at the water fearfully, and his head popped back up. "Somebody save me!" he screamed with all his might as he felt his body sinking again.

Suddenly, the lights snapped on in the house. Dressed in his pajamas, Paw Paw Chuck came running to the rescue. He had heard Cubby's cries for help.

But could he get there in time?

As Cubby was going under water for the third time, he remembered a Bible story about a man named Jonah. Once, Jonah had been sinking, too, all because he had disobeyed God. . . .

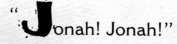

"Jonah! Jonah!"

The man sat up. When God spoke, Jonah listened.

"I have an important job for you to do."

"What is it, Lord?" Jonah could imagine all kinds of special assignments God would want him to do. He could lead a great army for God or speak to the king. Jonah could be a great lawyer or teach the royal children. Surely, it must be something great that God wanted him to do!

God interrupted Jonah's thoughts. "Jonah, I have a special message for you to deliver. I want you to go to Nineveh and make a special announcement."

Jonah's heart sank. "Oh, no! Please don't ask me to go to Nineveh, Lord," he pleaded. "I would rather go *anywhere* in the world, but Nineveh!" Jonah complained.

But God was determined. "Tell the people in Nineveh that I will punish them because they do not obey me."

Jonah did not want to speak to the people in Nineveh. But God had spoken clearly: "Go to Nineveh!" Jonah decided to disobey God. He thought to himself, *I'll just run away*.

Jonah sneaked out of town. He bought a ticket and boarded a ship headed in the opposite direction from Nineveh. (How far do you think Jonah got before God discovered this?)

Jonah fell asleep on the ship, thinking he was safe. Suddenly, a great storm struck. The wind howled and the rain beat against the ship. The sea became dangerous as the waves got bigger. The frightened sailors prayed to their gods of wood and stone. But their gods were not real. They could not hear or help. The sailors feared for their lives.

Meanwhile, Jonah was snoring in his bunk down below.

The sailors shook Jonah and said, "Wake up and pray that your God will save us!"

"I am a prophet of the living God," Jonah told the sailors. "My God made the heavens and the earth. He is the creator of the sea." Then Jonah confessed, "It is my fault that this terrible storm has come upon you. God is punishing you because of me. I have disobeyed Him."

The ship was about to sink, so the sailors picked up Jonah and tossed him into the water. At once the sea became calm.

God sent a big fish to swallow Jonah. After three days of living inside the big fish, Jonah learned how important it is to obey God. The big fish spit Jonah out of his mouth, and Jonah went to Nineveh.

Jonah spoke the word of God to the people there. The people of Nineveh believed his warnings and stopped doing evil things. They started living the way God's Word told them to live. Obedience paid off! God saved Jonah, and He saved the people of Nineveh, too!

Paw Paw Chuck jumped into the cold water to save Cubby. "Hold on, Cubby! I'm coming," he yelled. Paw Paw Chuck reached his strong arm into the deep water and grabbed Cubby's arm. With one arm holding Cubby close to his chest, Paw Paw Chuck swam toward the dock. He pulled Cubby out of the water and carefully propped him up on the dock. Cubby coughed and sputtered.

"Cubby! Are you okay?" Paw Paw Chuck asked.

"Yes, Paw Paw," Cubby said as he coughed, choked, cried, and shivered. "I'm sorry, Paw Paw. What Buzzy and I did was wrong. We should never have gone fishing at night. We disobeyed."

"It was my fault," Buzzy said softly. "This never would have happened if I hadn't talked Cubby into breaking your rules. I'm sorry, too."

Paw Paw Chuck nodded knowingly. "I forgive
you both," he said, as he wrapped the cubs in a big bear hug. "I'm
glad you learned your lesson. You learned tonight how important it is
to obey the rules. You know, we should always obey God's rules, even
when we don't understand why He tells us to do something. You can
obey God by keeping the rules I set for you or by cheerfully doing
what your parents ask you to do. Keep this in mind next time you're
asked to get ready for bed, or clean your room, or take out the
garbage. Cubs, obey your parents, for 'this is the right thing to do!'"

LOST & FOUND

A STORY ABOUT SALVATION

*"If you use your mouth to say,
'Jesus is Lord,' and if you believe
in your heart that God raised Jesus
from death, then you will be saved....
The Scripture says, 'Anyone who asks
the Lord for help will be saved.'"*

ROMANS 10:9, 13

"Remember, if you don't know how to 'snow plow' to stop, just drop your poles and plop!" Paw Paw Chuck said with a big grin.

Paw Paw Chuck was giving a quick ski lesson to some of his grandcubs before they braved the snow-covered peaks on Mammoth Mountain.

"Yeah! Let's go! Let's ski this slope!" Heather said playfully.

"Hey Parker, wanna race?" Chelsea asked her cousin.

"Last cub to the bottom of the hill is a grizzly," Parker pushed his poles into the powdery snow and slid past Chelsea. Little Landon hurried to catch up.

The day was a flurry of fun on the slippery slopes for Paw Paw Chuck and his grandcubs. But all too soon it was time to leave the winter wonderland and return to the cabin.

"Time to go, grandcubs," called Nana Cindy. "It's almost dark."

The grandcubs followed Paw Paw Chuck and Nana Cindy down the snowy path. The cubs looked like polar bears in their thick, arctic jackets and big boots. They crunched through the snow, carrying their equipment.

Parker's steps slowed to a shuffle as he tried to get one last glimpse of the mountain playground.

"C'mon, Parker!" Paw Paw Chuck called from the front of the furry pack. "You're falling behind."

"You better speed up, Parker," Ryan yelled.

While the bears stomped through the icy forest, Parker stopped to play. He threw himself into the snowdrifts. He made chubby snow angels. He plucked pine cones with his paws and pitched them to imaginary baseball players. Parker paused to watch the snowflakes fall to the ground. *Wow! There must be millions of them,* he thought.

The wind started to blow. The chill was almost more than Parker could "bear." He spotted a nice clump of fir trees. *I can stay warm there,* Parker thought. He curled up under the trees to rest, as the snow continued to fall. *I wonder if I'll be able to find my way back to the path?* Parker worried. *I sure hope my family isn't too far from here.* Parker's eyelids grew heavy as he thought about the lost lamb story that Paw Paw Chuck had told him.

Meanwhile, Paw Paw Chuck discovered that Parker was missing from the group.

Paw Paw Chuck saw that Nana Cindy and the other grandcubs were safely on their way to the cabin. Then Paw Paw Chuck returned to the snowy path to search for his lost grandcub.

"Parker . . . Parker!" Paw Paw Chuck called across the snowy paths and trails. He looked everywhere, but Parker was not in sight.

Paw Paw Chuck prayed, "Dear Lord, please keep Parker warm and safe on this cold, winter evening. Let me find him quickly before it gets too dark. I love him so much. Please, comfort Parker wherever he is."

In the clump of fir trees, Parker had fallen asleep. While he slept, he had a dream about a good shepherd. . . .

A good shepherd watched over many sheep. The shepherd loved his sheep. Each one was very special to him. He kindly cared for their needs and listened to their bleats.

The good shepherd protected his flock. He cautiously kept them from dangerous slopes, rough spots, and wild animals. The shepherd was very wise, very kind, and very careful.

Every morning, as the sun came up, the shepherd called his sheep together and counted them. He wanted to make sure that no one was missing from the flock.

The good shepherd called each lamb by name. "Snowball! Fluffy! Pinky! Chester! Where are you?"

"Baaa . . . baaaa . . ." the lambs bleated in quick reply.

While the shepherd was taking roll, he realized a lamb was missing from the fold. "Ninety-seven, ninety-eight, ninety-nine . . ."

Where was the last little lamb? Where was number one hundred? Maybe the sheep was sleeping.

The shepherd called the sheep by name, "Lambert! Lambert!" But the missing lamb did not answer.

The lamb must have wandered away from the flock. Why would the lamb leave his family and friends to travel the dangerous trails alone? Why would the little one stray from the good shepherd's loving care and protection?

The shepherd knew Lambert was in trouble. The shepherd knew the lamb was no match for the wolves that prowled the hills, or the bitter cold nights. The good shepherd left his ninety-nine other sheep and hurried out to search for Lambert.

Where is my little lamb? Is he hurt? Is he hiding from me? the shepherd thought, as he looked over the hills for the lost one. *My lamb will be frightened and worried. He will feel lonely without me by his side.*

"Lambert! Laaam . . . berrt!" the shepherd called. "Where are you?"

The shepherd searched high and low. He hunted many hours for the lost lamb. He combed through the brush. He climbed over hills and crawled through dark caves, calling for Lambert every inch of the way. Finally, he spied small sheep hoofprints. The shepherd followed the tracks. *Oh, no!* thought the shepherd. The tracks led away from the safe pastures.

At last, when it was almost too dark to see, the shepherd spotted Lambert caught in a thorny bramble bush. Very carefully, the good shepherd got him out of the bush.

"Baa . . . baaaa," Lambert cried. The lost sheep was tired, hungry, and cold. The shepherd lovingly carried the lamb in his arms. The good shepherd spoke kind words of comfort to his frightened little lamb. He picked him up and held him tightly to calm him.

The shepherd then carried the lamb back to the flock. "Look everyone!" he announced. "Lambert was lost, but now he is found!"

The ninety-nine sheep were happy. They praised the good shepherd for saving Lambert.

Where am I? Parker thought, as he awakened from his short nap.

The cub was scared. "I'm alone in the forest!" Parker cried. "Where is my family? Why didn't I stay with them?"

The moonlight "bearly" lit the darkness. Parker buried his snout in his paws and sobbed. Suddenly, he heard a familiar voice.

"Parker! Parker!" Paw Paw Chuck called.

"Paw Paw Chuck, I'm over here!" Parker yelled. Parker wiped the cold tears off of his furry face and waved at Paw Paw Chuck.

"Praise the Lord! I'm so glad I found you," Paw Paw Chuck called as he and Parker ran toward each other. "I've been looking everywhere!" Paw Paw Chuck wrapped his big arms around Parker. "I love you, Parker. I asked God to keep you safe. C'mon, let's go back to the cabin."

"Good idea, Paw Paw Chuck!" Parker squealed. "I have been out here in the cold for too long."

33

When Paw Paw Chuck and Parker opened the door of the cabin, all the other cubs came running.

"Oh, Parker! We're so glad you are here. We were worried about you," they said. Ryan, Chelsea, Heather, and Landon surrounded Parker and took turns giving him bear hugs.

Nana Cindy brought out some hot chocolate for everyone.

While the bears sat in front of a warm fire, sipping their hot chocolate, Nana Cindy said, "You know, I've been thinking about something."

"What's that, Nana?" everyone wanted to know.

"Well, just like Parker was lost out on that hillside today, there was once a time in our lives when we were all lost in sin. But Jesus, the Great Shepherd, came to find us. He is always looking for those who are lost. When we heard the voice of Jesus call to us, we answered, 'Jesus, please save us!' And Jesus did just that."

"I'm so glad Jesus loves us enough to come looking for us when we are lost," Heather said as she snuggled up close to Nana Cindy.

"And I'm so glad to be *found!*" Parker shouted.

"Me too . . . me too . . . me too," the other bears squealed.

"Amen!" said Paw Paw Chuck. "We're *all* glad Jesus found us!"

All the grandcubs listened quietly as Paw Paw Chuck explained how Jesus is always looking for those who are lost. They smiled as Paw Paw Chuck reminded them, "Anyone who asks the Lord for help will be saved."

GOOD NEWS BEARS

A STORY ABOUT TRUSTING GOD

*"When I am afraid,
I will trust You."*

PSALM 56:3

"Stee . . . rike three!" the umpire roared. "You're out."

Buddy sadly walked back to the bench.

"Hugh J. McGruff is too hard to hit," Buddy sobbed to his teammates.

McGruff howled with laughter.

He appeared almost frightening as he paced back and forth on the pitcher's mound.

It was the last inning of the big game. The score was tied and there were two outs. This was the Bears' last chance. Coach Clawson, the Bears' manager, scratched his head. Who could he put in to pinch-hit against the Tigers?

37

"Who wants to pinch-hit?" Coach Clawson asked, as he looked into the faces of the bears sitting on the bench.

"Not me," said Fuzzy. "Hugh J. is too big."

"Me neither!" cried Itchy. "McGruff is too fast."

Meanwhile, Hugh J. McGruff spat on the ground and cracked jokes about the Good News Bears.

"I will!" said a high-pitched voice. "Let me bat!"

"Oh, no! Not Landon!" the Bears growled.

Only six years old, Landon was the youngest and smallest member of the Good News Bears. In fact, he had "bearly" made the team. Most of the time, Landon carried a water bucket so the other players could get a cool drink.

"Doesn't anyone else want to bat?" Coach groaned.

Nobody made a sound as Hugh J. McGruff made nasty faces at the Good News Bears.

"I'll bat!" Landon said cheerfully.

Coach sighed, "Okay, Landon. You may as well strike out, too. Everybody else has."

Landon grabbed his bat and ran out to the batter's box. He kicked the dirt around with his "bear" paw, just as he had seen the big league bears do. Then he raised his bat over his shoulder, and he stared at Hugh J. McGruff.

McGruff laughed, "What's this little squirt doing in the game? Ha! Ha!"

Just then Landon caught a glimpse of Paw Paw Chuck sitting in the bleachers.

"Come on, Landon! You can do it!" Paw Paw shouted. "Don't be afraid. Size means nothing! Remember David and his slingshot!"

Landon smiled. He knew exactly what Paw Paw Chuck meant. He remembered the story of David and Goliath very well. . . .

GOOD NEWS BEARS VS. THE TIGERS

Along time ago, there was a battle between God's people and another army. In those days soldiers didn't have submachine guns or fighter planes. Instead, they fought their wars with spears and swords and clubs.

The other army—the bad guys—had a really scary giant who fought on their side. He was almost ten feet tall, and his name was Goliath. One day Goliath yelled, "Nobody is as tough and mean as I am! Send your best soldier to fight me. If I can kill him, the battle is over, and our side wins. If he whips me, you win."

Now, God's people were supposed to have lots of courage because God was on their side. But when they heard Goliath's voice, they were really scared! God seemed very far away, even though He really wasn't.

God's people had a king named Saul, and he was the leader of their army. "Anybody want to fight Goliath?" he asked hopefully. "I'll give a big reward to anybody who kills the giant. I'll even give you one of my daughters as a bride."

The soldiers glanced at each other. They were big and strong and well-trained fighters. But right then they were more afraid than anything else. And Goliath was at least ten times tougher than they were.

King Saul shook his head sadly. "I wish someone here wasn't afraid to try." (Of course, he didn't want to try either, but nobody mentioned that because he was the king.)

Just then a teenager named David walked up to King Saul. David said, "Don't worry about Goliath, King Saul. God will win for us. I will fight the giant for you."

The king was worried. And he was curious, too. He asked, "You're just a shepherd boy. What do you know about giants?"

David shrugged his shoulders. "I don't know anything about giants, but I do know something about God.

"God can take care of His people. Plus, I'm a pretty good shot with this," David grinned, pulling a slingshot out of his backpack. "I'm not afraid to take on this giant. Furthermore, as long as God is on our side, we can't lose!"

By that time, Goliath was stomping around in the middle of the battlefield, getting madder by the minute. "Come on out and fight! I'll take on anybody!"

"Okay, okay," King Saul said to David. "Give it a try." "And," he added, "the Lord be with you." So David trusted God as he marched out to face the giant.

Goliath was angrier than ever! "How dare you send that little pip-squeak out to face me!" he roared. He rushed toward David with his spear.

"You're fighting me with a sword and a spear," David shouted at Goliath. "But I'm fighting you in the name of the Lord! He makes His people strong!"

David quickly put a rock in his slingshot and sent it flying through the air. The rock was right on target. It hit the giant—SMACK!—in the middle of his forehead. With a great crash, Goliath fell to the ground.

Because a boy trusted God, God's people had won the battle!

Whoosh! The ball sped past Landon.

"Stee . . . rike one!" the umpire roared.

Hugh J. McGruff threw the ball again, this time even harder.

Landon was scared, so he prayed, "I am trusting You, Lord! Help me to do my best."

"Stee . . . rike two!" said the man in blue.

Landon heard Paw Paw's encouragement, "Remember David!"

With fresh courage, Landon blinked and stepped back in the batter's box as he gripped his bat tightly.

McGruff threw the ball one more time. . . . Landon swung with all his might.

Craa . . . ack! What a hit! The ball soared up, over McGruff's head.

"Going! Going! Gone!" Paw Paw Chuck cheered.

The ball kept climbing until it flew over the fence for a home run. The Good News Bears won the game.

As Landon rounded the bases, the Bears ran onto the field to greet him at home plate.

Fuzzy called, "How did you hit the ball so hard?"

Landon answered, "The Lord helped me."

Paw Paw Chuck hurried onto the field. "I knew you could do it!" Paw Paw smiled as he lifted Landon into his arms and gave him a great big Paw Paw bear hug.

The next time you're afraid of something or someone, remember how David trusted God and won the victory. Ask God to help you, too!

'ACCIDENTALLY' ON PURPOSE

A STORY ABOUT FORGIVENESS

*"Be kind and loving to each other.
Forgive each other just as God
forgave you in Christ."*

EPHESIANS 4:32

Chelsea was as sweet as she was pretty. She had big brown eyes with long eyelashes and golden-brown hair. Everyone at school loved Chelsea. Everyone, that is, except Pawla and Goldie. Pawla and Goldie were jealous of Chelsea because she was so pretty and popular.

One day, Chelsea wore a beautiful gold-colored jacket to school. It was a jacket that Chelsea's Granny-Bear Bonnie had made especially for her.

"Look at that jacket. It looks three sizes too small," Pawla teased.

"I liked your old jacket better," Goldie lied.

Even though they made her feel bad, Chelsea smiled kindly at the jealous bears.

"It must be nice," Pawla whispered later to Goldie. "My grandmother has never made me anything."

Later that day during art class, Chelsea took off her jacket and placed it over her chair. When Chelsea left the classroom to get a drink from the water fountain, Pawla and Goldie saw their chance to be mean.

"Let's spill some of our paint on Chelsea's new jacket!" Pawla said to Goldie.

"*Accidentally*, of course," Goldie replied with a mean laugh.

Just then, Chelsea returned to the room. She was almost back at her seat, when Goldie jumped up and purposely tipped over the big jar of red paint onto Chelsea's beautiful jacket. The paint spattered down the front of the jacket and quickly began to sink into the cloth.

"Oh, no!" cried Chelsea when she saw what had happened.

"Oops," said Goldie mischievously. "Oh, Chelsea, I'm sorry. The jar slipped out of my hand." Goldie lied.

"I'm sure it was an accident," Chelsea said quietly.

"Maybe your Granny-Bear Bonnie can sew you another jacket since this one is ruined," Pawla said, pretending to feel sorry for Chelsea.

"No," Chelsea answered. "This was a very special fabric Granny-Bear used. I don't think she will ever be able to make me another jacket like this one."

Suddenly, Pawla and Goldie felt bad about ruining Chelsea's jacket.

After school, Chelsea went to Paw Paw Chuck's house and showed him her paint-stained jacket.

"Chelsea!" he exclaimed. "What happened to your beautiful new jacket that Granny-Bear Bonnie made for you?"

"A girl at school spilled paint on it. She said it was an accident, but I think she ruined my jacket on purpose. I try to be nice, but she and her friend Pawla are so mean to me. And now my special jacket is ruined."

Paw Paw Chuck picked up the stained jacket. "Mmm," he said, "this looks bad. But let's see what we can do."

Paw Paw Chuck filled the sink with clean, cold water. He placed Chelsea's jacket in the water. Very gently, he began to rub the paint with berry soap.

Paw Paw Chuck emptied the sink and refilled it with clean water. Again, he gently soaked and rubbed Chelsea's jacket. Paw Paw Chuck repeated the process again and again while Chelsea stood close by, watching and hoping.

"I think that is the best we can do for now, Chelsea," Paw Paw Chuck said. "We will just have to let the jacket dry before we know for sure if the stains have come out. While we are waiting, I'll tell you a Bible story about some young fellows who were also jealous because of a jacket. . . ."

man named Jacob had twelve sons. Jacob loved all of his sons, but the son he loved the most was Joseph. All the brothers knew that Joseph was their father's favorite. This made the brothers very angry and jealous.

They grew even more jealous when Jacob gave Joseph a rare, colorful coat. Every time Joseph's brothers saw his coat, it reminded them of their father's special love for Joseph. The brothers became more and more jealous.

One day in the field, when Joseph's brothers saw him coming, they talked angrily with one another. "Let's kill him," they said. "We will drop him into a deep pit and tell our father a wild animal ate him."

Reuben, the oldest brother, was afraid. He tried to stop the others. "We must not kill our brother," he said. "Let's just throw him into the pit like a prisoner."

As soon as Joseph reached the brothers, they grabbed him, tore off his beautiful coat, and shoved him into an empty pit.

Then the brothers saw a group of traveling traders coming and decided to sell Joseph to them. The brothers knew that the traders would make Joseph a slave. Joseph would suffer much. But the jealous brothers didn't care.

As the traders left, the brothers must have wondered what they had done. Why had they been so jealous and cruel? How could they do this terrible thing? How could they be so mean? But it was too late.

The traders took Joseph to Egypt and sold him as a slave. Joseph worked hard and suffered much as a slave in Egypt. But God blessed everything he did.

Many years passed. Finally, Joseph was given the highest position in the land, next to the king.

One day, Joseph's brothers came all the way from Canaan to buy food.

They did not know they would have to buy their food from their long-lost brother, Joseph. They thought he had been dead for years.

All the brothers bowed down before Joseph, the governor of Egypt. The brothers had no idea who he really was.

Joseph, however, recognized his brothers. "Brothers, it is I, Joseph," he said.

The brothers were shocked! They were afraid that Joseph would punish them for selling him as a slave many years before.

"Don't be afraid of me," said Joseph. "I will never try to get even with you because I forgive you. God turned into good what you meant for evil."

Joseph told his brothers to move to Egypt so they would have plenty to eat. Jacob was happy when he heard that his son Joseph was alive. The whole family moved to Egypt. Jacob and his sons lived in peace together in Egypt for many years because Joseph chose to forgive.

Paw Paw Chuck put his big furry arm around Chelsea. He smiled gently as he said, "Chelsea, almost anyone in Joseph's place would have had those brothers punished for selling him as a slave. But not Joseph. He knew that God had a reason for everything. He realized that God had a bigger plan, so he forgave his brothers."

"That is a wonderful story," Chelsea said, as she snuggled closer to Paw Paw Chuck.

"Yes, it is," Paw Paw Chuck agreed. "But I was wondering, do you need to forgive some people for doing something mean to you?"

Chelsea looked up into the gentle eyes of her grandfather. "Do you mean Pawla and Goldie, the ones who tried to ruin my beautiful jacket?" she asked.

"Mmmm-hmm," Paw Paw Chuck answered with a nod.

"Yes, Paw Paw. I understand. I forgive Pawla and Goldie for spilling paint on my jacket. I forgive them for being so mean to me. I forgive them for being so jealous, too."

"Good," said Paw Paw Chuck. "Now let's see how your jacket is doing."

The next day at school Goldie said to Pawla, "Let's tell Chelsea we're sorry for ruining her jacket and ask her if we could help her clean the paint out of it."

"Yeah," Pawla said. "We were wrong to treat Chelsea that way."

Just then Chelsea came into class. Goldie and Pawla were surprised to see her smiling at them.

"Hi, girls!" Chelsea called. "Look! Almost all of the paint washed out of my jacket! Paw Paw Chuck helped me clean it. Isn't that wonderful?"

"It *is* wonderful!" Pawla answered with a big smile.

"Oh, Chelsea. We are so glad!" said Goldie. "We are sorry for being jealous. And we are sorry for trying to ruin your jacket. It wasn't really an accident when the paint spilled. I did it on purpose. Please, please forgive me."

"Yes," agreed Pawla. "I'm sorry, too. Please forgive me, too, Chelsea."

"I already have," Chelsea replied with a twinkle in her eye. "Have you ever heard the story about a man named Joseph? Let me tell it to you. . . ."

Chelsea told Pawla and Goldie the story of Joseph, just as Paw Paw Chuck had told it to her. Then Chelsea said, "See, you did something bad, but God used it for good. Look, now we are friends. Like Paw Paw Chuck always says, 'Good things happen when we forgive.'"

THE BUSY BEES

A STORY ABOUT
READING GOD'S WORD

*"All Scripture is given by God
and is useful for teaching and for showing
people what is wrong in their lives.
It is useful for correcting faults and
teaching how to live right."*

2 TIMOTHY 3:16

"Have a good day at school, Ryan," Paw Paw Chuck told his oldest grandcub. "I'll pick you up after school. Then we'll go straight to the soccer field. Tell your teacher, Mr. Blackbear, I said hello!"

"Okay! See ya later, Paw Paw," Ryan said, as he hopped out of the van and ran toward the school.

During science class that afternoon, Ryan noticed his friends Alvis and Arley. They were passing a note to one another while Mr. Blackbear talked to the students about queen bees and worker bees. Mr. Blackbear was not pleased with Alvis and Arley when he discovered what they were doing.

"Alvis Presley and Arley Davidson, would you like to share your note with the rest of the class?" Mr. Blackbear asked.

"No, sir," Alvis said.

Arley sat quietly.

"Throw away the note," said Mr. Blackbear. "Please, pay attention, boys. We were talking about the busy life of a worker bee." Mr. Blackbear continued his lesson.

"In each hive about 15,000 bees live together in a small apartment complex. The workers take care of their queen. The worker bees build, clean, and defend their home. . . ."

Arley tried to listen, but all that talk about beehives, honeycomb, and royal jelly made his stomach growl.

Mr. Blackbear interrupted Arley's thoughts. "Cubs, before recess you should finish reading the chapter in your book about honeycomb."

Arley did not read his book. Instead, Arley started daydreaming about the field next to the playground. *Hmmm,* he thought. *If I follow one of the "busy bees," I bet he'll lead me to some honey!* Arley rubbed his fuzzy tummy.

During recess that afternoon, Arley asked Alvis and Ryan, "Want to find some honeycomb and royal jelly?"

"I saw bees over there," Alvis said as he pointed over to the flower field. "Let's go!"

"No, thanks," Ryan said. "Didn't you read your chapter, Arley? A beehive is crowded with over 15,000 worker bees. Besides, we aren't supposed to leave the playground."

"We'll bring you back some honeycomb, Ryan," Alvis said.

Ryan's eyes grew wide with concern for his friends. "Be careful."

"We'll be right back," said Arley. He and Alvis ran to a wire fence around the playground. They quickly climbed over the fence and scampered through the field.

Alvis and Arley found a small bee on a flower blossom.

"Let's follow him home," said Arley.

"There he goes," Alvis said, as he ran after the little bee.

Alvis and Arley followed the bee to a large tree with a big hive in it. Arley's eyes sparkled with delight. Alvis smiled widely . . . "There it is."

"The hive is too high for either of us to reach, but I have an idea," said Alvis. "Climb up on my shoulders, Arley. Then you can grab the honeycomb for both of us."

Arley climbed up on Alvis's shoulders. He reached out to lift some honeycomb from the hive.

"BZZZZZZ . . . BZZZZZZZ . . . We're being attacked!" shouted a bee guarding the entrance to the hive. He sounded the alarm to all the other working bees inside the hive.

Suddenly, a swarm of angry bees went on the attack! Arley tumbled off Alvis's shoulders. Both raced through the field. They jumped over the fence and ran toward the school building. But they were not fast enough to outrun the angry bees. The bees quickly caught up with Alvis and Arley and stung them every step of the way.

"Ooooch! Ouch! Ooooch! Ouch!" Alvis and Arley growled.

"Help! Help!" they howled, unable to paw the bees away.

"Cubs, quick, get inside the school building!" Mr. Blackbear said to the students in the play area. He opened the school door for the cubs to enter.

The bees returned to their hive as Alvis and Arley ran inside the school building. Alvis and Arley moaned loudly because their bee stings hurt so much.

Ryan felt bad for Alvis and Arley. Their bearskin became swollen from the bee stings. "I'm sorry you got stung," Ryan said to his two friends.

Mr. Blackbear called Arley's and Alvis's parents.

Alvis's mom was very upset with him. "Wait 'til your father sees you. He is not going to be happy."

"You shouldn't have left the playground, Arley," said Mrs. Davidson.

Alvis and Arley were upset because they were in trouble and because their bee stings HURT!

Later, Paw Paw Chuck returned for Ryan. "How was your day?"

Ryan told Paw Paw Chuck all about Alvis, Arley, and the bees.

"I'm glad I listened to Mr. Blackbear and obeyed the school rules. I'm glad I read the book during science, too. It warned bears to stay away from beehives."

"Your science book told you important information that saved you from making a big mistake with the bees. But there's another book that has the most important information of all. Do you know what that book is?" Paw Paw Chuck asked with a grin.

"The Bible!" Ryan answered loudly.

"That's right," Paw Paw Chuck said. "Ryan, what you did today reminds me of a boy in the Bible named Josiah. Let me tell you about him. . . ."

Josiah was eight years old when he became king of Judah. He was a relative of King David who had lived hundreds of years before. Even though Josiah was very young, he decided to do good things and live right just like King David had done.

One day, King Josiah noticed that the temple of God needed repairs. He hired carpenters to rebuild the temple in Jerusalem. He wanted the house of God to be the beautiful place of worship that it had been long ago when King David's son Solomon had it built. King Josiah wanted the temple to be a place of honor and respect for God.

While the workers were busy repairing the temple building, they found an old scroll. To their surprise, it was the Holy Book that contained God's teaching. These Scriptures taught God's people how to live right.

When the carpenters gave the scroll to Josiah, he said, "I want to hear what God has told us." Josiah told his royal helper to read the Scriptures to him.

As Josiah listened carefully, he became upset when he heard the things God said in His Word. Most of the people in Josiah's kingdom were not following God's instructions or obeying His commands. King Josiah decided their bad ways had gone on long enough. The solution was to teach the people in his kingdom God's Holy Scriptures.

He invited all the people in Judah to the temple for a big meeting. Josiah read the Word of God to the people. The more he read, the sadder they became. They were sorry they had not known God's Word. They were disappointed they had disobeyed God. King Josiah and the people of Judah decided to obey God's commands and follow His rules from then on!

As King Josiah grew older, he led the people to serve the Lord. And God blessed Josiah for obeying His Word.

Paw Paw Chuck looked at Ryan and said, "It is important for us to study God's Word and obey His instructions, Ryan. The Bible will show you how to choose the best way to live. God loves you so much. God gave you His Word to help you make good decisions. That's why it is important for you to read God's Word—you must know what He has to say so you can do what He wants you to do."

Ryan smiled at Paw Paw Chuck and said, "From now on I'm going to read my Bible every day!"

THE AUSSIES ARE COMING!

A STORY ABOUT LOVE

*"Love your neighbor
as you love yourself."*

LEVITICUS 19:18

Several neighborhood cubs were spending the day with Heather while she visited Paw Paw Chuck and Nana Cindy.

"Hey Heather, come here! You've *got* to see this!" B. J. stared through the living room window with amazement.

"What is it?" Heather glanced toward the window.

Before B. J. could answer, a buzzer went off. Nana Cindy hurried to the kitchen to check the cookies she was baking.

"Looks like we've really got ourselves a different breed of neighbors this time!" Itchy growled.

Twelve-year-old Clawdette looked out the window. "Heather, quick! Come look at their wacky moving van."

"WHAT are they?"
Heather frowned.

"They're koala bears, and that one's a kangaroo," said Clawdette. "I'd say that they're fresh up from down under."

"Where's 'down under'?" B. J. was confused.

"Australia," announced Clawdette. "It's a big country on the other side of the globe."

"It's where the platypus and lizards and dingo dogs and crocodiles . . . and all kinds of strange creatures come from!" said Clawdette smugly.

The four cubs huddled closely around the window, wide-eyed and curious. They had never seen anyone from down under before.

Meanwhile, the Aussies continued to pound out a muddy path from their moving van to the front door of their new home in the United States.

"I wish I could be more helpful, Olivia," Pete Aussie said. Pete's fuzzy, little arm was in a sling. "Ya know, since my tree-house accident I haven't been able ta lift much."

Just then a big, brown kangaroo came bouncing through the yard with several boxes.

"Well, mate," LaRoo said, almost out of breath, "the front door'll have ta come off for sure!"

The cubs began to panic as Mr. Aussie and the kangaroo came bouncing up the path to Paw Paw Chuck's front door.

"They're coming up the walk!" Heather gasped.

"No way!" blurted B. J.

"They're too different from us!" cried Itchy. "I don't want to meet them."

DING . . . DONG! The doorbell rang suddenly.

"Will someone please get the door?" called Paw Paw from the basement.

"Not me." Itchy scrambled behind the couch with B. J. and Clawdette close behind.

"They're standing on our porch!" Heather shrieked as she bolted into the closet.

DING . . . DONG.

After several rings, Paw Paw Chuck came rumbling up the basement stairs.

"Where are those cubs, anyway?" he mumbled to himself as he cheerfully opened the door to greet the new neighbors.

"G'day, mate." The friendly koala bear stuck out a tiny paw as he spoke. "M'name's Pete. This 'ere's LaRoo 'n we're movin' up from down unda."

"Well, hello Pete. Hello, LaRoo. It's a pleasure to meet you both." Paw Paw Chuck smiled and

held out a friendly paw. "I'm Paw Paw Chuck. Won't you come in?"

"Well, mate," Pete replied, "We'd really like to, but I'm 'a-fride' we're in a bit of a fix."

"You see," LaRoo began to explain, "Pete 'ere fell out of the tree back home and broke his arm."

"Yes, 'n LaRoo has come ta help m'wife an' me move in," Pete continued. "He'll be gettin' back to Australia once we're all settled in."

79

"But we're havin' a time tryin' to haul the refrigeratar through the front door of the Aussies' new place," LaRoo interrupted. "So if ya've got a screwdrivar we just might be back in business."

"Why, certainly!" Paw Paw Chuck smiled. "You're more than welcome to borrow a screwdriver or any other tools you may need, for that matter. Give me just a minute and I'll fetch my toolbox."

Before Pete and LaRoo could spell "k-a-n-g-a-r-o-o," Paw Paw Chuck returned with his toolbox and a neighborly grin. "You just let me know if there is anything else you need," Paw Paw Chuck offered.

Pete and LaRoo waved good-bye.

"Thank ya, mate," Pete said with appreciation while LaRoo nodded. "Ya're very kind, sir."

"Just call me Paw Paw Chuck. Nana Cindy and I will look forward to having you over once you are settled in." Paw Paw Chuck smiled and waved as they turned to go.

"The pleasure will be ours, Paw Paw Chuck!"

The door closed with a loud thud.

"All right, cubs," Paw Paw Chuck's voice was firm. "I want each one of you little fuzzies to come out of your hiding places . . . right now!"

One by one the cubs slowly crawled their way to the open space in the living room.

"We need to have a talk," said Paw Paw Chuck. "I want to tell you a story that I learned when I was just a cub myself. It's about a big problem called *prejudice*—and a little something called *love*."

There once was a poor man from Judea who traveled from Jerusalem to Jericho. Along the way, he was attacked by a gang of dangerous robbers. They tore off his clothes, beat him up, and stole his money.

The poor man groaned as he lay bruised and bleeding by the side of the road. The robbers ran off and left him to die.

A priest from Judea walked by. He saw the wounded man lying in the road. The priest crossed over to the opposite side of the street. He did not want to get involved. Instead of stopping to help the hurt man, the priest quickly walked away.

Later, another leader from Judea walked by the wounded man. He saw that he was hurt, but he also ignored the man and walked by on the other side of the road.

At last, a man from Samaria came by and saw the injured man. Even though he wasn't from that area, the Samaritan felt sorry for the man and took care of him. He washed off the man's wounds, gave him a cool drink, then carefully placed the wounded man on his donkey. The Samaritan took him to a nearby inn and spent the night watching over him. Here the injured man could get well. The Samaritan gave the innkeeper some money to pay for the hurt man's care. "If it costs more," he promised, "I will pay you the rest when I return from my trip."

Paw Paw Chuck smiled and asked, "Now, which one of the three men was the best neighbor to the poor man?"

"The man from Samaria was the best neighbor," said Heather.

"That's right," said Paw Paw Chuck. "Jesus told His followers that the good Samaritan was the best kind of neighbor because he had love in his heart. You see, the Samaritan refused to let a different skin color or different sounding words stop him from loving and caring for someone in need."

"I feel bad for poking fun at our new neighbors," Itchy said, as he looked toward the window.

"Me, too." B. J. sighed.

"We shouldn't have made fun of the way they look," admitted Heather.

As the little koala bears struggled to get their refrigerator through their front door, Heather suggested, "Maybe we can help them!"

"That's a great idea, Heather," said Paw Paw Chuck.

Just then Nana Cindy came back into the room.

"I can help carry some boxes for them," offered Itchy.

"Nana Cindy, why don't you and I take some cookies to the new neighbors?" asked Heather.

Paw Paw Chuck hugged the cubs and said, "I'm so proud of you! Now you're beginning to understand what it means to 'love your neighbor as you love yourself.'"

'BARBEAR' SHOP QUARTET

A STORY ABOUT THANKFULNESS

*"Give thanks to the Lord
and pray to him. . . .
Sing to him. Sing praises to him.
Tell about all the wonderful
things he has done."*

PSALM 105:1, 2

"Fasten your seat belts," Paw Paw Chuck said as he shut the car door. The car was crowded with Quartet members. There was "bearly" enough space for him to squeeze behind the wheel.

"Is everyone here? Everybody have on a seat belt?" Paw Paw called to the passengers.

"Yes, sir," said Beryl. "We're ready to roll."

Paw Paw pulled out of the church parking lot. "Let's practice singing on our way to Happy Valley."

"Yeah!" came a joyful shout from the Boys' Quartet.

Happy Valley was a retirement center for the elderly bears in the community. The older grizzlies looked forward to the young bears' concerts once a month.

"Hey, Buddy, sing the melody to 'God Is So Good,' then we'll join in with our harmony parts," Alvis instructed.

A beautiful, acappella four-part harmony filled the car. The cubs continued singing their favorite songs. Paw Paw Chuck smiled as he listened to the lovely singing. Paw Paw added his rich "bearitone" to each song's ending.

Suddenly, a loud bang interrupted the singing. *BOOOOM!* Bump, bump a thump, bump . . . bump, bump a thump, bump. The car bounced to a grinding halt.

"Uh, oh! Looks like we got ourselves a flat tire," said Alvis.

"Quick! Everyone get out of the car," Paw Paw Chuck called to the boys.

Alvis and Beryl helped Paw Paw Chuck haul the spare tire out from the back of the car. All the cubs anxiously watched Paw Paw Chuck try to change the flat tire.

"Uh, oh!" said Alvis. "Looks like we got ourselves another flat tire!"

"Yep! That spare is flat as a pancake," said Beryl.

Paw Paw Chuck looked away from the disappointed cubs to the lonely highway.

"Alvis and I can walk down to the next exit to call for help," Buddy volunteered.

"Wait, Buddy," said Paw Paw Chuck. "Here comes a car!"

A shiny red car was coming. All the bears waved. The woman driving sped by, leaving the cubs with a sinking feeling.

They stood on the side of the road wondering what to do.

"Someone better go quickly for help," Itchy spoke up, "or we will miss the concert!"

Just then, a station wagon drove up. The driver slowed his car when he saw the cubs. Then he pulled off the highway and parked near Paw Paw Chuck's car.

A well-groomed gentlebear got out of the car and walked toward Paw Paw Chuck. "Hi! My name is Harry Ordinary. Is there something I can do to help?"

Paw Paw Chuck introduced himself to Harry, then showed him the flat tires.

"We were on our way to sing at Happy Valley, but I'm not sure we will make it now," Paw Paw Chuck explained to Harry.

"There is a gas station at the next exit, near my barber shop. I'll take your tires to be fixed. Then I'll call Happy Valley from my barber shop, if you'd like," Harry kindly offered.

"Thank you, that would be very nice of you," Paw Paw Chuck said.

"You stay with the cubs, and I'll be right back," Harry said as he walked toward his car with a tire under each arm.

Harry kept his promise. He quickly returned with the repaired tires. Then Harry and Paw Paw Chuck changed the tire and put the spare in the back of the car.

The cubs rushed to Paw Paw Chuck's car. They were in a hurry to get to the concert.

Paw Paw Chuck reached out to shake Harry's paw, "Mr. Ordinary, thank . . ."

BEEP! BEEP! The honking car horn interrupted Paw Paw's conversation with Harry.

Paw Paw Chuck turned to see which bear was honking the horn.

"C'mon, Paw Paw, we've got to go!" the cubs yelled. "If we are any later, the Happy Valley bears will be sleeping."

"I'll be there in a minute," Paw Paw Chuck said firmly. Again, Paw Paw turned to thank Harry, but Harry was driving away. Paw Paw felt sad that neither he nor the cubs had properly thanked Harry for his help.

Paw Paw Chuck drove to Happy Valley in silence.

After the concert, the elder bears thanked and praised the quartet for their show. But all the thanks that the cubs received just added to Paw Paw Chuck's guilty feelings. *I wish the cubs would have told Harry how much all of us appreciated his help*, Paw Paw thought.

During the drive home from Happy Valley, Paw Paw Chuck had a serious talk with the cubs. "Can you cubs name something that disappoints Jesus?" Paw Paw Chuck asked.

"Stealing berries!"

"Growling and fighting!" the bears yelled out.

"Yes, all those things make Jesus sad." Paw Paw Chuck paused. "But there is something else that disappoints Jesus. It's something we often forget to do. Let me explain. . . ."

Jesus was on His way to Jerusalem. Along the way He traveled through a small town.

Outside of this village sat ten men. They all had a serious skin disease. Their bodies were covered with ugly sores. Most people didn't want to go near these men. People were afraid of catching the awful disease. The men with the disease were forced to leave their families and friends.

When the men saw Jesus going to the city, they called to him, "Jesus! Please help us!"

Jesus felt sad when He saw the suffering men. He said, "Go and show yourselves to the priest."

The men rushed to the city. As they obeyed Jesus, a miracle happened—their sores went away. The men were so happy to be healed! They hurried to show their family and friends.

One man was different. When he saw that he was healed, he thought, *I must quickly thank Jesus for healing me.*

The man hurried back to thank Jesus. When he saw Jesus he bowed down and said, "Because of God, I'm healed." The man showed Jesus his skin. "Thank you for healing me, Master!"

"Ten men were helped. Where are the other nine?" Jesus asked. "Are you the only one to thank God?"

Jesus was disappointed with the nine men who were too busy to stop and thank God. But Jesus was very pleased with the one thankful man.

The bears sat quietly in Paw Paw Chuck's car.

"Paw Paw Chuck," Buddy spoke up, "I think we all need to 'paws' and thank God for sending Harry along to help us. We would have missed the concert without his help."

"That's a good idea, Buddy," Paw Paw Chuck said.

"I wish we would have thanked Harry for helping us," Alvis said sadly.

"Well, I think we still can thank Harry," Paw Paw Chuck said as he stopped the car in front of Harry's "Barbear" Shop.

The bears happily piled out of the car.

"Let's sing a song for Harry," Alvis suggested. "Let's show him just how much we appreciated his help." And that's exactly what they did!

Harry and his customers were delighted to hear the "barbear" shop quartet . . . and Harry was pleased they stopped to thank him.

Always remember to thank other people for nice things they do. Most of all, be sure to thank God for the good things He does for us over and over again.

WAITING FOR A WEDDING

A STORY ABOUT PATIENCE

"Wait and trust the Lord. . . .
Don't be upset;
it only leads to trouble."

PSALM 37:7, 8

"Smile!" said Mr. Jolly, the wedding photographer, as he flashed a picture of the bride.

"I can't believe our Colleen is getting married today," said Nana Cindy to Paw Paw Chuck. Nana Cindy wiped tears from her eyes.

"Yes, the years have slipped by quickly," Paw Paw Chuck whispered, squeezing Nana Cindy's paw. "Speaking of time, the ceremony will be starting soon."

"Aunt Colleen, you look beautiful," said Chelsea and Heather, who were excited about being junior bridesmaids. Charissa, Colleen's matron of honor, smiled in agreement.

TAP! TAP! TAP! A knock at the door interrupted the photo session.

The nervous groomsmen stood in the church hallway and waved to Paw Paw Chuck.

"Psst . . . Paw Paw, could you come here for a minute?" called Parker.

Paw Paw Chuck hurried to the hallway.

"We have a little problem," Landon continued.

"Look!" said Ryan. He pointed to Mark, Aunt Colleen's groom. "His tux is way too small. He can't even button the coat."

"It's almost two sizes too small!" Parker added.

"Oh, no. How did that happen?" Paw Paw Chuck asked.

Poor Mark looked sadly at Paw Paw Chuck. "By mistake, I picked up the wrong tux from The Handsome Grizzly Tuxedo Shop," Mark said, shaking his head from side to side.

Just then, Heather and Chelsea peeked into the hallway. Their eyes grew wide with surprise. "What can I do?" Mark worried. Paw Paw Chuck frowned as he looked at his wristwatch. A moment later he nodded his head and smiled.

"I have a plan," Paw Paw Chuck proposed. "If we work together, I think we can correct this little problem. I'll take Mark to the Tuxedo Shop to exchange his tux for a larger one. We should have just enough time to return to the church before the wedding begins."

Paw Paw Chuck explained the plan to Nana Cindy and Colleen. Colleen was worried. "Are you sure you will be back in time for our wedding?" she asked.

"Don't worry, Colleen—everything will be fine," Paw Paw Chuck reassured her. "We'll ride my Harley so we can zip through traffic." Paw Paw Chuck slipped on his gloves then put on his safety helmet and adjusted the strap. Mark followed Paw Paw Chuck to the church parking lot as he, too, strapped on his helmet.

As Paw Paw Chuck and Mark zoomed onto the highway, thunder rumbled across the sky.

Colleen and Nana Cindy glanced upward at a dark cloud.

"It's going to rain!" Colleen cried. "They'll get soaked on that bike!"

"The storm may hold off until after they return," Nana Cindy comforted her daughter.

"I hope they hurry," Colleen murmured.

"Let's wait inside," Nana Cindy suggested, as she led her daughter into the church waiting room.

Colleen slumped into a chair and started to bite her claws. She kept glancing at the clock on the wall. "I sure hope they hurry," she mumbled to herself.

"Be patient," her mother said. "They'll be back soon."

"Poor Aunt Colleen," whispered Chelsea.

"How can we help her?" Heather asked her cousins.

Colleen stood up and started to pace back and forth.

"Please sit down and relax," Nana Cindy said. She smiled lovingly at her daughter.

Colleen sat on the edge of the couch and wiggled one paw nervously. "They aren't going to make it back here in time for the wedding. They are going to get drenched in a rainstorm. Oh . . . I wish they would hurry!" Colleen said anxiously.

"Colleen, after waiting a lifetime for the right husband, twenty minutes is a short wait." Nana Cindy sat calmly on the couch near her daughter, trying to encourage her.

Heather whispered, "Let's tell Aunt Colleen a story."

"Which story?" Ryan asked.

"Paw Paw Chuck's story about patience!" Chelsea answered.

"Great idea," said Ryan. "Who is going to tell the story?"

The cubs pointed to Ryan. "You are!" they agreed.

Colleen looked at the cubs. "I would love to hear a good story right now," she said gloomily. "It will help take my mind off my worries."

Ryan told the story to Aunt Colleen the way Paw Paw Chuck had told him. . . .

Martha loved to have friends for dinner. She carefully planned each meal. She was very organized. She worked hard to prepare the food. But the problem was, she worried about every detail. She wanted everything to be perfect.

Martha and her sister, Mary, especially enjoyed having their good friend, Jesus, in their home. And Jesus liked to visit with them and their brother, Lazarus.

One time, while Jesus was visiting in their home, Mary became so interested in Jesus' words that she decided to stop everything and sit down to listen to Jesus talk. She learned many things through the stories He told. Mary was always encouraged by Jesus' words.

As Jesus told a story to Mary, Martha continued working in the kitchen, alone. Martha waited for her sister to return to the kitchen. After a while, Martha became upset. She began to fret. She wondered why Mary was not helping her prepare the meal. Finally, Martha became very impatient.

She thought, *Where is Mary? What is taking her so long? I need her to help me! Why is she wasting time while I do all the work? I wish she would hurry back to the kitchen.*

Finally, Martha looked into the room, and to her surprise, there was Mary sitting at Jesus' feet! Martha could hardly believe her eyes. She decided to speak to Jesus about Mary. She marched in and blurted out, "Lord, don't you care that I have to do all this work by myself, while Mary is sitting here doing nothing? Tell my sister to get up and come back to the kitchen and help me."

Jesus surprised Martha with His words. He said, "Martha . . . Martha, please stop worrying! Be patient. You are upset over too many little things. Mary is doing the right thing. She's sitting here listening to Me, and that's exactly what she should be doing . . . and so should you!"

As Ryan finished telling the story, Colleen giggled, "Your Paw Paw has told me that same story many times. I need to stop worrying and start trusting God when I feel anxious and nervous. I need to practice patience instead of worrying."

"Aunt Colleen, we can pray that God will help you feel better, too," Heather suggested.

Colleen nodded her head. "Mom, will you pray for me?" Colleen asked.

"Certainly." Nana Cindy prayed for Colleen, "Lord, allow Colleen to enjoy her wedding day. Help her to stop worrying about all the little details. Help her to wait patiently for Mark. Thank You, Father, for hearing our prayer. Oh, and Lord, would You please keep the storm away a little longer so Paw Paw Chuck and Mark don't get wet? Amen."

Just then, Paw Paw Chuck's big blue and black bike came roaring into the parking lot.

"Yippee! They're back!" the cubs cheered.

"Whew! We still have five minutes before the wedding song begins," said Colleen as she looked at the clock.

Colleen kissed her mother and whispered, "Thanks for being patient with me."

Just as the rain began to fall, the back door opened wide. It was Paw Paw Chuck with a big grin on his face! "Your handsome groom has arrived on time and in a tuxedo that fits perfectly. And not one hair got wet," Paw Paw exclaimed as he entered the room.

Colleen hugged her father before peeking into the sanctuary where Mark stood waiting patiently for her. Colleen whispered to Paw Paw Chuck, "Well, he is worth waiting for, and that tuxedo looks terrific! Thank you for your help, Dad."

Paw Paw Chuck hugged his daughter. He then looked at Nana Cindy and smiled. "It's time for the wedding to begin," he said. He held out his paw, and the mother of the bride took his arm as he escorted her to her seat. Then he returned to walk the bride down the aisle, but first he put his big furry arms around her. "What a wonderful day this will be, sweetheart!" He whispered in her ear . . . "Never forget, Colleen, when we wait on the Lord, He rewards our trust. I'm learning more and more that patience always pays off!"

SHARE BEARS

A STORY ABOUT SHARING

*"It is more blessed
to give than to receive."*
ACTS 20:35

Paw Paw Chuck had finished mowing the lawn while baby Noah slept soundly. The baby was strapped in a baby carrier to Paw Paw's back. Nana Cindy was out of town, and Paw Paw was looking after Noah while his momma and daddy, Jeni and Chuck, were gone for the afternoon. Paw Paw Chuck was enjoying a glass of cold lemonade that warm spring afternoon.

The school bus stopped in front of the Brown's house. Paw Paw Chuck waved at Clawdette, B. J., and Itchy.

"Hi, Paw Paw Chuck! Can we come over for a while?" the cubs shouted.

"Sure," Paw Paw Chuck said in a half whisper so he wouldn't wake up baby Noah. "In fact, your mom had to run a couple of errands and asked me to watch you until she returns."

The three little bears raced to Paw Paw Chuck's front porch. "I can hardly wait 'til our baby sister or brother is born," said Clawdette, as she looked at Noah sleeping in the baby carrier.

"I hope it's a girl cub," said B. J. "Then Clawdette will have to share her room with the new cubby."

"Yeah," Itchy moaned. "Our room's too small for another boy cub."

"That isn't true," Clawdette protested. "You have plenty of space in your room. You just don't want to have a baby cub sleeping near you."

"Clawdette, cribs are not cool!" B. J. complained.

"Our friends will tease us if they find out we're sleeping in a nursery!" Itchy whined.

Just then baby Noah began to cry.

"Can I hold Noah?" Clawdette asked.

"Sure," Paw Paw Chuck said. He carefully placed the baby in Clawdette's arms. Noah immediately stopped crying. He looked up at Clawdette with his big blue eyes and smiled a toothless grin.

"I think he likes me!" Clawdette exclaimed.

"He is a cute little guy," B. J. said.

"His paws are so tiny!" Itchy added.

Paw Paw Chuck chuckled. "Before long you guys will enjoy being big brothers."

"And big sister!" Clawdette chipped in as she put Noah in his stroller.

B. J. and Itchy smiled at the thought of having their own baby brother or sister. Then another thought struck them.

"But won't we have to give some of our toys to the new cub?" B. J. was concerned.

"Yeah, and we probably won't get as much stuff for Christmas, either," Itchy added, "because there will be four cubs in our family instead of three."

B. J. and Itchy frowned at each other. Clawdette just rolled her eyes.

RING! RING! RING!

Paw Paw Chuck hurried inside the house to answer the telephone. When he returned, Paw Paw Chuck had a big smile on his face. "How would you cubs like to have dinner with baby Noah and me tonight?" he asked.

"That sounds like fun," Clawdette squealed.

"But we'll have to ask Mom and Dad first," B. J. cautioned.

Paw Paw Chuck laughed. "Let me explain. That call was from your dad. Your mother went to the hospital this afternoon. The doctor said the baby cub will probably be born this evening! So your parents want you to stay with Noah and me for a while."

"Yipee!" Clawdette shouted.

"I wonder if it's a boy?" B. J. asked excitedly.

Paw Paw Chuck grinned at the excited cubs. Then he took a deep breath and said, "Well, while we are waiting for the news about the new baby, let's get dinner started."

The Brown bears followed Paw Paw Chuck into the kitchen. As Paw Paw Chuck began looking through the cupboards, he realized he hadn't gone to the grocery store since Nana Cindy had been out of town. The cupboards were almost bare!

"Cubs, the only things I can find for dinner are baby food and these spaghetti noodles." Paw Paw Chuck frowned.

"Maybe we have a jar of spaghetti sauce at home," B. J. suggested.

"Hey! If we put our sauce and your noodles together, we can make spaghetti," said Clawdette.

"I'll run home to check," Itchy volunteered. A few minutes later, Itchy returned with a jar of spaghetti sauce.

Paw Paw Chuck quickly made the spaghetti while the cubs washed up for dinner. When they finally sat down to eat, they said a prayer of thanks for the food. Then Paw Paw Chuck said, "This dinner reminds me of a little boy in the Bible who shared his meal with others. I will tell you the story while we eat. . . ."

One day, Jesus was teaching a large crowd on a hillside. It was time for lunch, and the people were very hungry. There was no place nearby where they could buy something to eat.

Jesus asked Philip, "Where can we find enough food to feed all the hungry people?"

Philip answered, "We don't have that much money. We would have to work many months to earn enough money to buy even a little snack for all these people."

A young boy had come to hear Jesus speak. He had packed a small lunch. In his basket were five loaves of barley bread and two small fish. The young boy wanted to share his lunch, so he gave his little food basket to Jesus.

Jesus' close followers said, "Lord, there will not be enough food for everyone. Should we send the people home?"

Jesus replied, "Tell the people to sit down on the hillside. We are going to have lunch together." Jesus prayed over the meal. He thanked God for providing the bread and the fish. And He asked God to bless the food in the basket.

Jesus then told His disciples to take the food and share it with the hungry crowd. God blessed the meal as Jesus performed a mighty miracle. Everyone on the hillside had plenty to eat . . . and there were thousands there that day! After everybody had eaten, there were still twelve basketfuls of food left over!

After dinner, Paw Paw Chuck said, "What a great meal we had because we shared!"

Just then the telephone rang.

Paw Paw Chuck quickly reached for the phone. "Hello? Oh, that's wonderful! I'll tell the cubs."

"Well, cubs, only a few minutes ago, a brand-new boy cubby was born to the Brown family!" Paw Paw laughed with joy as all the cubs jumped up and hugged each other. "His name is Curly!"

"Oh, I can't wait to hold him!" Clawdette said excitedly.

B. J. and Itchy smiled at each other. "Looks like we'll have to share our room with the little bear after all," Itchy said to his brother.

"I won't mind sharing my space or my toys with our new brother," B. J. said.

"Neither will I," agreed Itchy. "I think it will be fun to share our room with little Curly."

Paw Paw Chuck winked at the three bears. "It's always fun to share," said Paw Paw Chuck. He reached down and picked up his tiny grandcub and held him close. "Isn't that right, little guy?"

Noah smiled another big toothless smile. "That means 'Right!'" said Paw Paw Chuck.

THE PINEWOOD DERBY

A STORY ABOUT TRUTHFULNESS

*"So you must stop telling lies.
Tell each other the truth. . . ."*
EPHESIANS 4:25

Cubby loved Frontier Cubs. He looked forward to the weekly meetings in the church gym. He had learned many new things, like how to build birdhouses and make kites. He especially liked the Bible stories that Mr. Tom or Paw Paw Chuck told the troop.

"Okay, boys!" Mr. Tom called to Frontier Cubs Troop #77. "Everyone take a seat."

Cubby scrambled for a seat next to Buzzy and Fuzzy while Mr. Tom uncovered a large table filled with fancy little cars.

"Wow!" the cubs began to buzz with excitement.

"Listen up, cubs!" Mr. Tom continued. "For those of you who are new to our troop, these cars are made of pinewood. Each car was carved by bare paws."

Cubby's eyes grew wide with wonder.

"Now, cubs, let me tell you about the Pinewood Derby Race." Mr. Tom carefully explained, "You will receive a Pinewood Derby kit tonight. Inside each kit you will find a block of pinewood and four plastic wheels. Your job is to make a car that can race in the derby four weeks from tonight." Mr. Tom paused. "Now, it's very important to remember one thing—you must make these cars by yourself."

Paw Paw Chuck stood near Mr. Tom. He commented with a nod, "This means no help from your fathers, brothers, or older friends. You're on your own . . . and on your honor."

Paw Paw Chuck then handed a Pinewood Derby kit to each cub.

"Good luck, boys!" said Mr. Tom.

"Yes, and have fun building your car!" added Paw Paw Chuck.

"I'm gonna win the race this year. It's a cinch!" Buzzy growled after the troop meeting. "My dad is an engineer. He knows exactly how much my car should weigh to make it go faster than the others."

"Big deal," said Fuzzy. "My dad has a woodworking shop in the garage. When we get finished with my car, it'll leave yours in the dust!"

"What kind of car is your dad building for you, Cubby?" asked Buzzy.

"Well . . ." Cubby stuttered a bit and tried to find words to answer. He did not have a father bear living at home.

"Ummm, well, my dad has to work a lot, and I don't see him very much," said Cubby.

"That's too bad," said Buzzy.

"Oh, well," said Fuzzy. "Maybe you'll have a shot at winning the race next year."

"Next year?" asked Cubby with a frown.

"Well, how do you expect to win the Pinewood Derby Race if your father can't help you?" Fuzzy replied.

"I don't know," said Cubby, "but Mr. Tom and Paw Paw Chuck made it very clear that we are not supposed to let anyone help us make the cars. They were serious. I could tell by Paw Paw's frown."

"C'mon, Cubby," said Buzzy. "Do you really think every cub here is carving his own car out of a block of pinewood? Get real!"

"You really are new to this troop, aren't you!" said Fuzzy with a grizzly chuckle as they left the church gym.

For the next several weeks before the big race, many of the father bears and big brothers pitched in and helped build the Pinewood Derby cars for their cubs.

Meanwhile, Cubby worked on his Pinewood Derby car alone. Each day after school, Cubby whittled away at the wood until the block began to take shape. He sanded the wood until his little paws were tired. Finally, the car was shaped the way Cubby wanted it. He decided to paint it bright blue. He also painted a black racing stripe down both sides of the car. Cubby finished his car by snapping on the wheels. He was so pleased . . . and he had done it all by himself.

"Oh, Cubby," cried Cubby's mom, Berrie, the night of the big race. "Your car is beautiful."

"Thanks, Mom," Cubby grinned with pride. "I painted it your favorite shade of blue."

Later, in the church recreation room, the cubs showed off their Pinewood Derby cars.

"The race will start in fifteen minutes," Mr. Tom announced. "Paw Paw Chuck will help me weigh each car before the race."

The cubs made a beeline for the scales.

"Hey, Fuzzy, what do you think of my 'green machine'?" Buzzy asked.

"Wow, Buzzy, your car design is great," Fuzzy laughed. "My car isn't as bright, but it moves like lightning."

"Cubby, your car isn't too bad," Fuzzy grinned. "It should make it through the race."

Paw Paw Chuck smiled at Cubby as he weighed the small racecar. "Cubby, it looks like you did a fine job building this car. The weight is perfectly balanced, too," Paw Paw Chuck winked at Cubby. "I think you have a winning 'blue racer.'"

Cubby nervously placed his racecar next to the other handsome cars on the track.

"And now, let the Pinewood Derby Race begin!" Mr. Tom called out.

The crowd cheered loudly for their favorite cars.

"Go, Buzzy!" Buzzy's father and brothers yelled.

"Yea, Fuzzy!" Fuzzy's family were all there to see him win.

"C'mon, Cubby!" Berrie cheered for her son.

Cubby was proud of his blue car even if it looked rough next to the other cars. *It may not be as great as the other cars, but at least I followed the rules. I made my car all by myself,* Cubby thought. As he watched the pinewood cars scoot down the track, Cubby remembered a story about honesty that Paw Paw Chuck had told the Frontier Cubs Troop several weeks earlier. . . .

A man named Barnabas owned a field. He sold his property and gave the money to the church. They thanked and praised Barnabas for his generosity and thoughtfulness.

At the same time, another man named Ananias and his wife Sapphira sold some land. They were willing to give some of the money to the church, but they did not want to give all of the money away. Most of all they wanted to be praised for doing a good deed. They wanted everybody to think they were giving everything they had . . . but they weren't. They wanted honor without honesty.

Many believers were selling their land and giving all the money to the church. Ananias and Sapphira did not want to look less generous than their friends.

"What should we do?" Sapphira asked Ananias. "Our friends may think we are selfish if we don't give all our money to the church."

"We won't tell them how much profit we made from the sale," Ananias answered, with a sly grin. "Everybody will think we've given all, but let's only give a part of our earnings. We'll secretly keep some of it for ourselves."

"Isn't that a lie?" Sapphira asked her husband.

"Well, I'd rather think of it as a half-truth," Ananias snickered.

When Ananias and Sapphira stood before the church leaders to give their gift to God, the Lord did not find their half-truth funny.

"Why did you think you could lie and get away with it?" Peter said. "God knows all things. He sees the evil in your heart. The Lord is not pleased with your dishonesty."

God punished Ananias and Sapphira for their lies. Both of them fell over dead. This was God's way of announcing that there cannot be honor without honesty.

Just then, Cubby's "blue racer" shot past the other cars on the track. Cubby's eyes grew wide with excitement.

Berrie jumped up and down. "Go, Cubby, go!" she shouted.

Cubby's car whizzed down the race track.

"Cubby, you won the race!" Berrie cheered. "Yea, Cubby, you're the winner!"

Cubby looked at his mother and laughed. He could hardly believe he had won!

"Congratulations, Cubby!" Mr. Tom announced. "You are the official winner of this year's Frontier Cubs Pinewood Derby Race!"

The crowd clapped loudly for Cubby.

Paw Paw Chuck handed Cubby a large trophy. "I told you that car was perfectly balanced. I'm so proud of you, Cubby," Paw Paw Chuck grinned.

"How did you build such a fast car?" Buzzy whispered to Cubby.

"Yeah, what's your secret?" Fuzzy was puzzled.

"I don't have any secrets, guys," Cubby smiled as he proudly displayed his trophy to the cheering crowd. "I just obeyed the rules and built the car by myself!"

CUB-SITTING

A STORY ABOUT BEING FAITHFUL

*"If we are not faithful,
he will still be faithful. . . ."*
2 TIMOTHY 2:13

"Good-bye, Paw Paw Chuck," said Bernice Brown. "Good-bye, Nana Cindy. Don't worry. Clawdette will help me take care of your grandcubs while you are at the radio station."

"Thank you, Bernice," said Nana Cindy as she hugged her grandcubs. "Now, Ashley and Austin, you obey Mrs. Brown and help her take care of your baby cousin Noah. Paw Paw Chuck and I will return as soon as the radio show is off the air."

"We don't expect to be gone very long," said Paw Paw Chuck.

"Bye, Nana Cindy," said Ashley.

"Bye-bye, Paw Paw," said Austin as he waved his fuzzy paw high in the air.

Bernice put baby Noah in a crib for his nap. Then she turned to Ashley and Austin, her eyes filled with excitement. "If you cubs will follow Clawdette and me into the backyard, you'll find a big swing set and lots of toys!"

"Yeah!" Clawdette agreed. "We'll have lots of fun."

"Let's go!" Ashley shouted and grabbed her brother's paw.

"Yippee!" said Austin with a furry grin.

Clawdette was twelve years old, and she loved to cubby-sit.

"Wow!" Austin squealed at the sight of the big swing set in Bernice's backyard.

"Let's swing!" Ashley shouted.

"C'mon!" Clawdette called for the cubs. "I'll push you!"

"Wheeeeeeeeeeee!" Austin giggled as he swung back and forth.

"Higher! Higher!" he laughed with glee while Clawdette pushed him back and forth.

RING . . . RING . . . The telephone rang inside the house.

"Clawdette," Bernice called to her daughter.

"Yes, Mom." Clawdette came skipping through the yard with a tiny tape player fastened to her belt.

"Will you keep an eye on Ashley and Austin while I go inside and answer the telephone?" Bernice asked.

"Sure, Mom!" Clawdette answered. "No problem!"

Clawdette reached around to adjust the sound on her tape player. Clawdette loved her tape player. She loved the way it fastened to her belt. She loved the way the headphones fastened to her ears. And she especially loved to listen to the music that it played. Clawdette's favorite song, *Bakery, Bakery,* began to play.

Clawdette began to sing along with her favorite vocalist Aimee Durant. "Bakery, bakery . . ." Claudette left the play area to dance alone on the patio. As she sang and danced, she forgot to watch Austin and Ashley.

Meanwhile, Ashley started to climb the ladder to the tree fort.

"Hey, Austin!" Ashley squealed with excitement. "Look at me!"

"No, no, Ashley!" Austin gasped at the sight of her on the ladder.

But his sister climbed higher and higher until . . . suddenly, she missed a step and lost her balance. Ashley was falling.

"H-E-L-P!" she roared, all the way to the ground . . . *THUMP!*

Ashley lay on the ground crying, but Clawdette did not hear her. The music was too loud in Clawdette's ears. She continued dancing on the patio.

Bernice was just coming out the back door when she saw Ashley on the ground.

"Ashley! What happened?" Bernice shrieked as she ran toward the injured cub.

She lifted Ashley to her feet and wiped the tears from her fuzzy face.

Just then, Clawdette came running. "Oh, no!" cried Clawdette. "Ashley are you okay?"

"Her head has a big bump and there's a cut on her knee! She'll need a bandage for sure!" Bernice's voice was shaking. "Clawdette! I thought you were going to keep an eye on these cubs for me!"

"I'm sorry, Mom!" Clawdette began to cry. "Really, I am! I guess I wasn't paying attention."

"I guess you weren't!" Bernice said firmly.

"I feel better," said Ashley. She stopped crying and started to rub her head.

Bernice took care of Ashley's cut. Then she asked the cubs, "How would you like some homemade ice cream?"

"Yeah!" the cubs squealed with delight.

Clawdette took Ashley and Austin to the picnic table on the patio.

While Bernice served the cubs ice cream, Clawdette turned on the radio. Paw Paw Chuck's radio show had just started, and his voice could be heard loud and clear on the radio.

Bernice said, "It sounds like he's telling a Bible story about faithfulness...."

Many years ago there lived an evil king in Egypt called Pharaoh. Pharaoh hated God's people. He was afraid that one day soon there would be so many people living for God that they would outnumber the Egyptians and then overthrow his army.

"I'll see that the Hebrews never take my kingdom away from me!" cried Pharaoh. "I'll have every Hebrew baby boy thrown into the river!"

At the same time, a good Hebrew man and woman had a baby son. They were worried for their son's life because of the evil king's new rule.

"I have an idea!" said the baby's mother, "We'll hide our baby boy, and the king's soldiers will never find him!"

So, the couple hid their newborn son for three months. But as the baby grew, it was hard for them to keep him a secret. When they could no longer hide the baby, his mother thought of another way to keep him away from the evil king. She made a basket out of bulrushes so that it would float safely in the water. She knew Pharaoh's men would never think to look in the river. She placed the baby inside the special basket.

"Father in heaven," she prayed, "watch over my son and keep him from all harm." Then she put the basket in the water near the river bank.

The baby's older sister, Miriam, hid nearby to watch and make sure that the basket floated safely in the water. Miriam loved her baby brother. She knew it was her job to keep an eye on the basket in the water.

Miriam was faithful to look after her baby brother. Soon the daughter of Pharaoh came down to the river.

"I think I'll take my bath now," said the princess as she dipped her foot into the river.

Suddenly, she saw the little basket in the distance.

"Fetch me the basket from the water!" she said to her servant girl. "I wonder what's in it?"

"Waaaaaaaaa!" The baby's cry broke through the air as Pharaoh's daughter looked into the basket! What a discovery!

"This is one of the Hebrews' children!" the princess said with great surprise. "And what a beautiful baby he is. I think I'll keep him!"

Miriam came out of hiding and ran to the princess. She bowed low and said, "I know someone who can take care of the baby for you!"

"Bring her to me," Pharaoh's daughter replied wisely, "and I will pay her to take care of him."

Miriam went and got her mother. Miriam's mother cared for the baby until he was old enough for the princess to look after him. Then, she took the baby back to the princess.

"I think I'll call him 'Moses,'" said the princess, "because I lifted him out of the water."

So Moses grew up in the Egyptian palace. The princess loved him as though he were her very own son. Moses grew up to become a strong and godly leader. God later used him to lead his people, the Hebrews, into freedom. What a great hero he became!

Bernice said, "Clawdette, can you imagine what might have happened to Moses if his sister Miriam had not been faithful to watch over him?"

"I'm sorry that I wasn't faithful to keep an eye on the cubs, Mom." Clawdette frowned and shook her furry face from side to side. "It's a lesson that I never will forget."

Bernice smiled warmly at her twelve-year-old daughter.

Later, Paw Paw Chuck and Nana Cindy returned to pick up their grandcubs.

"How are my little cubs?" asked Paw Paw Chuck.

"Well, we need to explain what happened, Paw Paw," Bernice answered. "Ashley slipped and fell. . . ."

"But I'm okay!" said Ashley.

"I'm afraid it was my fault," Clawdette confessed. "If I had been more faithful to look after the cubs, Ashley would not have fallen."

"Well, it looks like she is doing just fine," said Nana Cindy with an understanding smile.

"You know," Paw Paw Chuck spoke kindly, "at one time or another, we all have failed to do something we should have done. Sometimes it takes a day like today to remind us just how important it is to stay faithful."

"You're right, Paw Paw Chuck," Clawdette agreed, "just like Miriam was faithful to watch after Moses in the Bible."

"We listened to your radio show," Bernice said with a smile.

"The story about Miriam is especially important," Paw Paw Chuck nodded as he spoke. "You see, God blessed Miriam and her whole family because she was faithful. And He promises to bless all of us when we are faithful. In fact, there are times He blesses us, even when we aren't faithful . . . even when we fail to do what we are supposed to do."

Nobody understood that better than Clawdette.

A STORY ABOUT LIFE AFTER DEATH

*"Jesus said . . . 'I am the resurrection
and the life. He who believes in me
will have life even if he dies.
And he who lives and
believes in me will never die. . . .'"*

JOHN 11: 25, 26

DING-DONG . . .
DING-DONG . . .

Paw Paw Chuck rang the doorbell of Great-Granny Bear's cottage while Nana Cindy, Ryan, and Chelsea stood next to him and waited.

Suddenly, the front door swung open wide.

"Hello, Paw Paw Chuck and Nana Cindy." Great-Granny Bear's nurse, Bearlinda, spoke softly.

"Hello, Miss Bearlinda," said Paw Paw Chuck and Nana Cindy.

"How is Great-Granny Bear?" asked Paw Paw Chuck.

"Not so good," Bearlinda explained. "She ate only a small bowl of blueberries this morning. That's the first thing she's eaten in several days."

"May we see her now?" asked Nana Cindy.

"You may indeed," said Bearlinda. "Great-Granny Bear is looking forward to your visit. She will be happy to see her great-grandcubs, too. Please follow me."

Bearlinda led the family through the tiny house. As the bears followed Bearlinda through Great-Granny's kitchen, they remembered many happy times.

"It seems like just yesterday we were celebrating Great-Granny Bear's 80th birthday," Paw Paw Chuck said, as he looked at the family pictures hanging on the wall.

Great-Granny Bear's bedroom was filled with letters, cards, plants, and photos from her great-grandcubs.

"Hello, loved ones," Great-Granny Bear spoke.

"Hello, Granny." Paw Paw Chuck took Great-Granny Bear's paw and kissed her cheek.

"How are my cubs?" Great-Granny Bear asked. As she spoke, Granny's dentures made little clicking sounds.

The cubs greeted Granny with smiles and kisses.

"We brought you something, Great-Granny Bear," said Ryan.

"And we picked them ourselves!" Chelsea added.

"Flowers!" Great-Granny Bear's face lit up for a brief moment. "You know I love honeysuckle!"

Granny squinted her tired eyes as she looked at the bears around her bed. "I'm so glad you came to visit today. I wanted to see you before I leave," Great-Granny Bear said with a twinkle in her eye.

"Before you leave?" Chelsea asked.

"Where are you going, Great-Granny Bear?" asked Ryan.

"I'm going to a place that I've dreamed of since I was a little cub," replied Great-Granny Bear.

"Can we go with you?" asked Chelsea.

"In due time, cubs," Great-Granny Bear nodded her head. "At the right time."

"Is that a long time?" Ryan questioned Granny.

"Not as long as it seemed when I was your age, my dear," Great-Granny Bear chuckled. "But you know . . . someday we can all be together again."

"Great-Granny Bear is going to heaven to be with Jesus very soon," Paw Paw Chuck explained.

"Does that mean you're not coming back?" asked Chelsea.

"Well, I thought I was gone this morning," Great-Granny Bear laughed. "But when I finally do leave, I won't come back!"

"Oh, Great-Granny Bear," Nana Cindy said. "You're such an inspiration."

"I'm going to miss you!" said Chelsea with a tear in her eye.

"And I shall miss you, little one," said Great-Granny Bear. "I have something to give each of you."

"See that quilt? It was stitched by my mother with her bare paws," Great-Granny Bear explained. "I want you to have it, Chelsea."

"Thank you, Granny!" cried Chelsea. "It's beautiful!"

"The tools in that box were your Great-Grandpa Bear's. He built this cottage with those tools. Ryan, I want you and Landon to share them," Great-Granny Bear said.

"Thanks, Granny!" Ryan said. "I can't wait to show them to Landon."

"Cindy, you're such a wonderful blessing to this family," Granny said. She sat up very slowly. Her fur was completely silver. "I want you to have my antique china."

"Oh, Great-Granny Bear, thank you for giving me such a special gift. I will treasure it always," Nana Cindy spoke softly. "I will give it to my grandcubs someday."

Chelsea said with amazement, "Granny's china must be a hundred years old. . . ."

" . . . And then some," Great-Granny Bear spoke up. "I can 'bearly' remember a Christmas dinner without it. When I was a cub, I watched my grandmother paint the blueberries on each dish."

"Chuck," Great-Granny Bear slowly held out her paw and continued to speak, "once I leave, I want you to have my Bible."

"It would be an honor, Great-Granny Bear," Paw Paw Chuck replied.

"But first," Great-Granny Bear took a deep breath, "I would like to tell one of my favorite stories to the cubs. Please fetch my Bible from the nightstand," Granny instructed.

The family gathered near the aging silver bear. They listened closely as she read from the book of Matthew. . . .

On Sunday morning, two days after the death and burial of Jesus, some women went to His tomb. At dawn, there was a great earthquake. An angel of the Lord came down from heaven. The angel went to the tomb and rolled the stone away from the entrance. Then the angel sat on the stone. His clothes were white as snow. He was shining brightly.

The soldiers guarding the tomb were frightened. They shook with fear. They fell to the ground like dead men.

The angel said to the women, "Don't be afraid. I know that you are looking for Jesus, the One who was killed on the cross. But He is not here. He has risen from death, as He said He would. Go quickly! Tell His followers, 'Jesus has risen from death.'"

The women left the tomb. They ran to tell Jesus' followers what had happened.

Suddenly, Jesus met them and said, "Greetings!"

The women fell to their knees. They felt afraid and happy at the same time.

Jesus said, "Don't be afraid. Tell my followers they will see me again."

After Jesus appeared to the women, He appeared to His followers many times. When Jesus' followers gathered together in Galilee, He told them, "Go make followers of all people in the world. Teach the people to obey my words. And you can be sure that I will be with you always."

Later, Jesus led His followers to the Mount of Olives. He lifted up His hands and blessed them. Suddenly, He began to rise in the air, higher and higher. A cloud covered Jesus and He went up to heaven.

While Jesus' followers looked heavenward, two angels appeared. The men said, "Why do you stand looking up into the sky? You saw Jesus taken away from you into heaven. He will come back in the same way you saw Him go."

Several weeks later, Paw Paw Chuck, Nana Cindy, and the cubs returned to Great-Granny Bear's house. They were packing Granny's belongings in boxes, since she had moved to her heavenly home.

Paw Paw Chuck found Great-Granny Bear's Bible on her nightstand. With it was a note. "Look, Cindy! Great-Granny Bear left me a note."

"What does it say?" asked Nana Cindy.

Paw Paw Chuck picked up the tattered, old Bible and read the scribbled handwriting on the piece of paper:

> Remember to share these great stories
> from the Bible with everyone you meet!
> Love,
> Great-Granny Bear
> P.S. I can hardly wait to see you again!